MY TURN! YOUR TURN!™

Goldilocks and the Three Bears

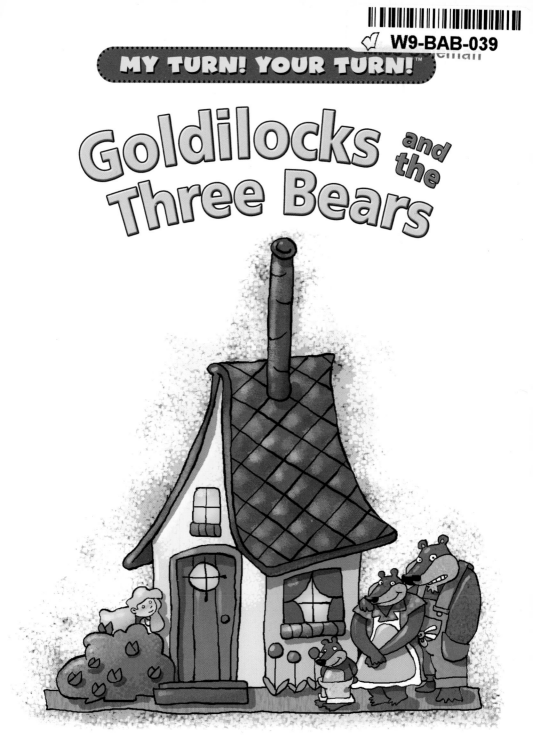

by Timothy S. Donehoo
Illustrated by Marcelo Elizalde

Guide for Parents

As your child's first teacher, you are instrumental in helping him or her become a reader. My Turn! Your Turn! readers are designed to support you in guiding your emerging reader. Your child can learn skills necessary to read by reading aloud with you!

The skills needed for reading include word recognition, text comprehension, vocabulary, and fluency. Fluency is the ability to read with accuracy, speed, and expression. Rather than reading word by word, fluent readers group words into meaningful chunks. They pause at the right time and read aloud with expression. The more fluent the reader, the better she or he comprehends.

My Turn! Your Turn! readers use child-adult repeated oral reading practice to increase these important skills. "Parent pages" on the left-hand side move the plot along. "Child pages" on the right-hand side contain repetitive, rhyming, easy-to-remember sentences, so your child meets with reading success. And early success with books helps your child become a good reader. Through repeated read-alouds, your child reads predictable, patterned text aloud several times per book, which will help to increase reading fluency. Your positive feedback guides your child's performance. Children

who reread passages orally as they receive feedback and praise become better readers.

My Turn! Your Turn! readers provide:
- Familiar tales that will engage your child.
- Clear, appealing illustrations that provide clues about the story.
- Simple designs that help familiarize your child with print.
- Predictable sentences that are repetitive, patterned, and often rhyming. Before long, your child will recognize familiar words.
- The opportunity to spend quality time together.

Before reading a My Turn! Your Turn! book for the first time:
- **GET COZY.** Find a comfortable, quiet spot to read together.
- **SHOW THE COVER.** Have your child talk about the picture. Read your child the title and author's name.
- **TAKE A "BOOK WALK."** As you flip through the pages, look at the pictures and talk about them. (You might say, "Let's see who the characters on the cover meet. Where does it look like they are going?")

Reading the book:

- **MODEL FLUENT READING.** For a first reading, read through the entire book aloud. Read naturally and expressively, as if you were speaking. This helps your child learn how a fluent reader sounds.
- **MATCH PRINT TO SPOKEN WORDS.** Place your finger below each word to help your child follow along.
- **ASK QUESTIONS.** Challenge your child to predict what will happen next.
- **ENGAGE YOUR CHILD IN REPEATED ORAL READING WITH GUIDANCE.** After one or more readings, invite your child to take a turn. Model how to read your child's page, then read it together. Ask your child to reread it the way you did. Provide help and encouragement.

When it's your child's turn to read:

- **HAM IT UP!** Suggest that your child use different voices for different characters' dialogue.
- **SET UP SUCCESS.** The last lines on the parent page are set in italics. When you come to these lines, use them to prompt your child to read his or her part by saying the first few words in a manner that lets your child know it is time to take over.
- **OFFER HELP.** If your child gets stuck on a word, you might say, "Could this word be 'straw'?" or "Look at the picture. What word makes sense?" If he or she is still stuck, provide the word, so comprehension is not interrupted.
- **PRAISE YOUR CHILD.** Compliment fluent reading and effort. Before you know it, your child may want to read the entire book independently!

After reading:

- **TALK ABOUT THE BOOK.** Have your child select a favorite part. Encourage a retelling of the story as your child looks at the pictures.
- **READ THE BOOK OVER AND OVER.** The more your child rereads, the more his or her accuracy, expression, and confidence will increase.
- **CREATE A BOND.** Use My Turn! Your Turn! readers for your child to share with a grandparent. Or suggest a read-aloud where your child and an older sibling alternate pages while the rest of the family listens.
- **BE A READING ROLE MODEL.** Seeing you read will have a positive effect on your child's attitude toward reading.*
- **READ TOGETHER DAILY.** Try to read at least 20 minutes a day. There is a direct relationship between reading skills and time spent reading.**
- **MOST OF ALL, HAVE FUN READING!** The more fun you both have reading, the more likely your child is to read!

Footnotes:
*According to the National Institute for Literacy
**According to the National Assessment of
  Educational Progress

Once upon a time in a cozy little house in the
deep dark woods there lived three bears.
The great big Papa Bear.
The middle size Mama Bear.
The little bitty Baby Bear.

The great big Papa Bear.

The middle size Mama Bear.

The little bitty Baby Bear.

Early one bright and sunny morning, the three bears sat down at the big table to eat a bear's breakfast. Papa Bear took a great big bite of his porridge. Mama Bear took a middle size bite of her porridge. And Baby Bear took a little bitty bite of his porridge.

"My porridge is too hot!"
"My porridge is too hot!"
"My porridge is too hot!"

"My porridge is too hot!"

"My porridge is too hot!"

"My porridge is too hot!"

So, the three bears decided that they would take a walk in the deep dark woods while their porridge cooled. The great big Papa Bear, the middle size Mama Bear, and the little bitty Baby Bear put on their warm clothes.

The great big Papa Bear put on his great big hat.

The middle size Mama Bear put on her middle size hat.

The little bitty Baby Bear put on his little bitty hat.

The great big Papa Bear
put on his great big hat.

The middle size Mama Bear
put on her middle size hat.

The little bitty Baby Bear
put on his little bitty hat.

Meanwhile, Goldilocks, a little girl with golden hair, was chasing her puppy in the deep dark woods.

"Please stop, puppy! I've been running so long. I'm hungry and tired," Goldilocks cried. Just then she saw the three bears' house. The door was open, so Goldilocks went inside...without being invited.

Goldilocks saw the three bowls of porridge on the table. One great big bowl. One middle size bowl. And one little bitty bowl. Goldilocks was so hungry that she could not stop herself from taking a little taste.

"This porridge is too hot!"
"This porridge is too cold!"
"This porridge is just right"

"This porridge is too hot!"

"This porridge is too cold!"

"This porridge is just right"

And Goldilocks ate it all up! Poor little bitty Baby Bear!

With her tummy full, Goldilocks walked into the living room to look for a place to sit. She found three chairs. One great big chair. One middle size chair. And one little bitty chair. Goldilocks was so tired that she could not stop herself from taking a seat.

"This chair is too hard!"

"This chair is too soft!"

"This chair is just right!"

"This chair is too hard!"

"This chair is too soft!"

"This chair is just right!"

And it broke into little bitty pieces! Poor little bitty Baby Bear!

Goldilocks brushed herself off and climbed the stairs to the bedroom. She found three beds. One great big bed. One middle size bed. And one little bitty bed. Goldilocks was so sleepy that she could not stop herself from lying down.

"This bed is too hard!"

"This bed is too soft!"

"This bed is just right!"

"This bed is too hard!"

"This bed is too soft!"

"This bed is just right!"

And Goldilocks fell sound asleep! Poor little bitty Baby Bear!

When the three bears returned from their walk in the deep dark woods they were as hungry as bears. On the table were three bowls. One great big bowl. One medium size bowl. And one little bitty bowl. But something was not right!

"Someone's been eating my porridge!"

"Someone's been eating my porridge, too!"

"Someone's been eating my porridge! And
    ate it all up!"

"Someone's been eating
  my porridge!"

"Someone's been eating
  my porridge, too!"

"Someone's been eating
  my porridge! And ate
  it all up!"

Papa Bear and Mama Bear gave Baby Bear a bear hug. Then the three bears walked into the living room to see what they could see. In the living room there were three chairs. One great big chair. One medium size chair. And one little bitty chair.

"Someone's been sitting in my chair!"

"Someone's been sitting in my chair, too!"

"Someone's been sitting in my chair! And broke it all up!"

"Someone's been sitting in my chair!"

"Someone's been sitting in my chair, too!"

"Someone's been sitting in my chair! And broke it all up!"

Papa Bear and Mama Bear gave Baby Bear a
bear hug. Then the three bears walked upstairs
to the bedroom to see what they could see. In
the bedroom there were three beds. One
great big bed. One medium size bed. And
one little bitty bed.

"Someone's been sleeping in my bed!"

"Someone's been sleeping in my bed, too!"

*"Someone's been sleeping in my bed! And
  she's still there!"*

"Someone's been sleeping in
my bed!"

"Someone's been sleeping in
my bed, too!"

"Someone's been sleeping in
my bed! And she's still there!"

The three bears gathered around Goldilocks as she lay sleeping. Suddenly, Goldilocks woke up and saw three bears looking at her. Without a word Goldilocks sprang from the bed, climbed out the window, and down the trellis. She ran out of the deep dark woods and all the way home with her little puppy chasing after her!

And never again did Goldilocks go into a house that was not hers without being invited.

The end!

The end!

This book belongs to:

_____

_____

My Turn! Your Turn! is a trademark of the Meredith Corporation.

ISBN: 0-696-22854-8

We welcome your comments and suggestions. Write to us at:
Meredith Books, Children's Books
1716 Locust St.
Des Moines, IA 50309-3023.
Or visit us at: meredithbooks.com